Rudi

Travels the World

by Nairy Shahinian

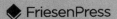

FriesenPress

Suite 300 - 990 Fort St
Victoria, BC, V8V 3K2
Canada

www.friesenpress.com

ISBN
978-1-5255-9983-5 (Hardcover)
978-1-5255-9982-8 (Paperback)
978-1-5255-9984-2 (eBook)

1. Juvenile Fiction, Animals, Dogs

Distributed to the trade by The Ingram Book Company

Table of Contents

Thank you to my loving family
who support me and believe in my
desire to create the opportunity
for children to read, learn,
imagine and dream.

Thank you Timur Deberdeev, for
your artistic talent and creativity.
...Every story comes alive with
your illustrations.

Thank you Marcy Drimer-Vidal
for your support, enthusiasm and
input in every editing detail.

CHAPTER 1

Summer Holidays

The summer holidays had finally begun! School was out, and Jazzy and Krik were very happy and excited! It was going to be a great summer, filled with lots of activities and adventures.

Jazzy and Krik's beloved goldie-poo, Rudi, was happy too. She was going to have fun with them all summer! Rudi knew it was going to be the best summer ever.

One morning, while everyone was happily discussing what their daily activities were going to be, Daddy called Jazzy and Krik into the kitchen for a family meeting. Family meetings were always held in the kitchen. It was the heart of the home where important things were discussed, and all sorts of decisions were made around the kitchen table.

Rudi was excited to be a part of the meeting. She followed Jazzy and Krik into the kitchen. Daddy had some ideas that he wanted to share with everyone. Rudi hoped that she would also be part of the family's summer plans.

Everyone was excited to hear what Daddy had to say. They all knew it was going to be a summer of fun, but also a summer of imaginary adventures for Jazzy, Krik, *and* Rudi.

"Jazzy and Krik, Mommy and I have a great idea for you," said Daddy.
"During your summer holidays, you are going to read and learn about
different places all around the world and the interesting animals that live
there. It will be an exciting way for both of you to learn about different
animals and their surroundings. It will be *so* much fun studying how these
animals live and interact with humans and how they make our world an

interesting and exciting place! You will need to make some trips to the library for all the books and maps."

Rudi was listening to Daddy very carefully. She already had so many wonderful friends. Rudi loved her doggie friends at the park, the neighbourhood squirrels, the happy birds that sang every morning, and the tiny bunny rabbits that had been born in the spring just outside the front porch. Now Rudi became excited to learn about *other* animals that she had *never* met before. She could hardly wait! Rudi did not know for sure what this exciting and fun-filled summer would be like. She did know that she was going to be happy to go wherever Jazzy and Krik were going.

Jazzy and Krik agreed with Daddy that during their summer holidays they would not only learn about different places and animals but also *visit* their natural habitats. Mommy took the big world map and placed it right above the fireplace in the family room.

Their imaginary summer "journey around the world" would begin in a few days. There was a lot to do, and everyone had to get ready! Everyone except for Rudi. Rudi still did not know if she was going with them. *Oh well*, Rudi thought. I guess *I'll find out tomorrow*. It had been a long day, and she was ready for bed.

"Sweet dreams, Rudi," said Krik. Tonight, she would dream about joining Jazzy and Krik on their wonderful summer adventure.

The next few days went by very quickly. The big world map above the fireplace was now outlined with a long dotted line. Jazzy and Krik had carefully planned out their route for the different and exciting places they were going to read and learn about. They had also added on colourful pictures of the animals that they were going to meet.

By now, Rudi was pretty sure that she was going to be included on this imaginary trip. Jazzy and Krik packed their bags, including one

4

for Rudi. They knew it was *very* important to have everything ready, especially when travelling to different countries. They had decided that their "journey around the world" would begin in the beautiful treehouse that Daddy had built for them a few summers ago. It was the best treehouse, full of big windows and comfortable pillows for them to sit on and dream the day away. It also provided lots of shade for them to keep cool during the hot summer months. Best of all, the treehouse was built so that Rudi could also enjoy it because it had a big ramp that she could easily climb.

The treehouse was the perfect place for Jazzy and Krik's *imaginations* to take flight.

Early the next morning, Jazzy, Krik, and Rudi went into the backyard and climbed into the treehouse. They were all ready to begin their exciting adventure around the world! Jazzy and Krik had already decided upon the words that they would repeat three times at the beginning and at the end of each imaginary journey. From their treehouse, the three of them were going to "travel" to amazing places, make new friends, and learn lots of new things. Rudi was especially excited because she was going to meet and learn about different animals from all around the world.

Jazzy and Krik were ready to repeat the special words three times. They closed their eyes, held hands tightly, and shouted,

"GO, RUDI… GO, RUDI… GO, RUDI…"

When they opened their eyes, they were at the bottom tip of the Arctic Ocean in Alaska! Their first adventure had begun and they knew it was going to be amazing!

CHAPTER 2

Alaska and the Humpback whales

Jazzy, Krik, and Rudi began to take in the sights and sounds of the Arctic Ocean. They noticed a fishing boat with a sign on it that said in big, bold letters, **"Welcome to Alaska"** and **"Whale Watching."** They quickly ran over to the boat and saw a familiar face. It belonged to a man wearing a bright yellow jacket and a red cap. He had big blue eyes and a white beard. On his jacket was a name tag that read "Captain Henry," and right beside his name was a picture of a humpback whale.

Captain Henry spotted Rudi and the children and shouted, "Welcome aboard! We're leaving in a few minutes to see the humpback whales! They're waiting for us!"

Jazzy, Krik, and Rudi quickly jumped aboard the fishing boat. This was going to be the most *exciting* boat ride! Jazzy and Krik had learned about humpback whales in school, and they had seen many pictures. But Rudi had never seen a whale before, except for the squeaky toy whale that she had at home.

They put on their life jackets and off they went with Captain Henry. He was a good friend of Jazzy and Krik's father and would make sure that

they all stayed safe. He was even going to teach them all about humpback whales and Alaska!

On the boat, Jazzy and Krik began looking out at the ocean with their binoculars. Suddenly, Rudi started barking excitedly. She ran back and forth and happily wagged her tail. Soon, they all saw what had made Rudi so excited. It was a pod of humpback whales! They were black with white markings, flippers, and flukes. Captain Henry explained that humpback whales were very powerful swimmers and that they mostly used their massive tails and fins, which were called "flukes," to propel themselves through the water. "When whales want to communicate with other whales," said Captain Henry, "they push themselves out of the water and leap into the air, making a huge splash when they land back in the water. This is known as breaching."

"What do whales like to eat?" asked Krik.

Captain Henry explained that humpback whales loved to eat shrimp, also known as "krill," and different kinds of small fish. Rudi wondered what shrimp tasted like. She had never eaten shrimp herself. *I'm sure they taste very good,* she thought.

"How much do whales weigh?" asked Jazzy. "They are *huge!*"

"The adult female weighs thirty-five tons, and the male is slightly smaller," replied Captain Henry.

Captain Henry then told them that it was the best time of the year to go whale watching. "In Alaska, the best months are June, July, and August," he explained.

"Alaska also has many other interesting animals, such as orcas—which belong to the dolphin family—mountain goats, moose, and caribou. Alaska has over one hundred thousand glaciers, and people can see the northern lights two hundred and forty days of the year. Alaska is also the largest state in the United States of America," he said.

On their way back to the dock, they saw many pods of humpback whales enjoying the crisp, cold waters of the Arctic Ocean. Up into the air and

down they leapt, always landing with a huge splash. They looked happy and free. It was truly a magical sight.

When they arrived back at the dock, the children thanked Captain Henry for their wonderful and exciting day. Jazzy, Krik, and Rudi were leaving Alaska with many wonderful memories. Captain Henry said goodbye and invited them to come back soon. He promised them that next time, he would take them to see the dolphins!

It was time for the three of them to return home. Jazzy and Krik closed their eyes tight and repeated the special words,

"GO, RUDI... GO, RUDI... GO, RUDI..."

When they opened their eyes, they were back in their treehouse. They soon heard Mommy calling them from the kitchen, "Jazzy, Krik, Rudi, dinner is ready!"

Boy, was there ever *a lot* for them to talk about at dinner. They could hardly wait!

CHAPTER 3

Canada and the Polar Bears

The next morning, Jazzy and Krik began their day by organizing their rooms, putting away their books and clothes, and getting their chores done. Although it was their summer holidays, they had promised Mommy and Daddy that they were going to keep their rooms clean and tidy. They had also promised to help Mommy and Daddy whenever they needed some help around the house.

After breakfast, Jazzy, Krik, and Rudi were ready for their next exciting and *imaginary* adventure. They made their way up to the treehouse carrying books, maps, snacks, and drinks.

Jazzy said, "Are we ready?"

Rudi barked happily in response and began wagging her tail excitedly. The children held hands, closed their eyes tight, and yelled,

"GO, RUDI... GO, RUDI... GO, RUDI..."

This time, they were off to see the polar bears by the western shores of Canada's Hudson's Bay—the world's capital of polar bears!

They opened their eyes and looked around. What they saw was a vast landscape illuminated by white snow. While they were admiring the view,

they noticed a group of tourists closely following a tour guide. He was holding a large flag with a picture of a polar bear on it. Everyone looked happy and very excited. The tour guide spotted Rudi, Krik, and Jazzy and asked them if they wanted to join the group.

He said to them, "You'd better hurry if you want to see the polar bears, we'll be on our way in a few minutes!"

Happily, Jazzy, Krik, and Rudi approached the tour group. The tour guide greeted everyone with a warm smile and said, "Hi, I'm Ranger Bob. Welcome to Hudson's Bay! Today, our group will be visiting our world-famous polar bears. Welcome aboard!" Jazzy, Krik, and Rudi were so excited! They climbed onboard the tour bus with the others and settled in their seats. Jazzy and Krik had *never* been on a bus like this before. Rudi had never even been on a bus before. She immediately jumped on a seat and got comfortable in-between Jazzy and Krik.

Once everyone was comfortably settled, Ranger Bob explained that they were actually riding on a tundra buggy.

"The tundra buggy is a heavy, bus-like vehicle that travels the roadless tundra easily. You will notice that the windows are extra-long for viewing the wildlife, and there is also an open deck for those of you willing to brave the cold."

Jazzy and Krik grinned happily at the idea.

At home, Rudi *loved* going on car outings with the family. This trip would be almost the same thing, except the tundra buggy was much bigger—and had bigger windows, bigger seats, and really big wheels. It was going to be a very exciting day! The first thing Rudi wanted to do was go out onto the open deck, but she had to wait until they got closer to the polar bears first. Rudi always *loved* the cold air and crisp winter breezes.

The tundra buggy started moving slowly. The passengers looked out the windows and saw Hudson's Bay, which was spectacularly beautiful and sparkling with snow drifts. It looked just like a winter wonderland! They were off to see the polar bears. Hopefully, they would also spot some Arctic foxes and wolves along the way.

Jazzy and Krik had lots of questions for the friendly and knowledgeable tour guide. Ranger Bob was very happy to answer them all. Jazzy had always wanted to know why polar bears were white. Ranger Bob explained that polar bears had white fur so that they could easily camouflage themselves in their environment.

"Their coat is *so* well-camouflaged," he said, "that sometimes they look like snow drifts. They also have a thick layer of body fat, which keeps them warm while they are swimming."

Krik wanted to know what polar bears liked to eat. Ranger Bob explained that polar bears were carnivorous, which meant that they liked to eat meat.

"They hunt for seal," he said, "because they also need large amounts of fat to be able to survive the cold."

There was a family sitting next to Jazzy, Krik, and Rudi. They had been listening to Ranger Bob's explanations with great interest. The little boy leaned forward to ask how polar bears hunted for seal.

Ranger Bob was very impressed with all of their questions. He explained to the little boy that the polar bears hunted for seal by keeping perfectly still on the ice and close to the seal's breathing hole.

"Sometimes, the polar bear has to wait for hours or *days* for a seal to pop up!" Ranger Bob laughed.

Rudi loved to swim and wondered if polar bears were good swimmers. Ranger Bob then began to describe polar bears as talented swimmers that paddled with their front paws and used their hind legs as rudders.

"The polar bears' paws are slightly webbed, which helps them swim. They are classified as 'marine mammals' because they spend most of their lives on sea ice and depend on the ocean for survival," he explained.

Ranger Bob then told them that polar bears always tried to keep as clean as possible because it helped them stay insulated from the cold. "After feeding, polar bears like to go for nice, long swims and clean themselves by rolling around in the fresh snow," he continued.

That certainly sounded familiar to Rudi. She *also* loved to play and roll around in the snow on her winter walks with Daddy.

Jazzy thought of another question for Ranger Bob. "How big are polar bears?" she asked. She could hardly believe it when Ranger Bob replied that polar bears were about the size of an adult guinea pig when they were born.

"The mother polar bear gives birth to twins, known as 'cubs,' and the cubs live with their mother for a little over two years. The bears live on ice-covered waters and hunt for seal. The adult male polar bear weighs about eight hundred pounds while the female weighs about four hundred pounds," Ranger Bob explained.

They are huge, thought Jazzy.

Ranger Bob finished his story by telling them how important it was to learn as much as possible about polar bears so that they could be kept safe from extinction.

As he was talking, the passengers, who had been looking out of their windows, began yelling excitedly, "Look! Look out there! *Look!*"

Outside the windows were two polar bear cubs. They were rising up on their hind legs and taking small steps towards each other. They were also playing and trying to wrestle each other! Jazzy, Krik, and Rudi were amazed. They had never seen anything like it before. The cubs were actually playing and having fun!

On the way back in the tundra buggy, they passed a couple of Arctic wolves and foxes. What a wonderful day it had been with Ranger Bob! But it was time to go home. When the tour was over, the children thanked Ranger Bob and promised that they would be back again soon.

It was once again time for Jazzy and Krik to close their eyes tight and repeat the happy words,

"GO, RUDI... GO, RUDI... GO, RUDI..."

When they opened their eyes, they were once again back in their tree-house. Their journey to northern Canada had been awesome, but very tiring. They were all happy to be home. Jazzy and Krik were also very hungry, and poor Rudi was exhausted. They left the treehouse and smelled the yummy hamburgers that Daddy was preparing on the grill.

"Daddy!" they yelled. "Do *we* have a lot to tell *you!* Wait till you hear about the polar bears and Ranger Bob!"

CHAPTER 4

Florida and the Sea Turtles

The summer holidays were always the best time of the year to have fun with family and friends. The next morning, Krik asked Mommy and Daddy if his good friend, Alain, could come over and spend the day at their house. Alain and Krik had been friends since they were little. Krik, Jazzy, and Rudi were very excited that Alain would be coming over. Alain knew all about the trio's daily adventures and was very excited that he was also going to be a part of them.

After breakfast, the four friends ran outside and climbed into the tree-house. They made sure that they had everything they needed for their next adventure. Rudi waited impatiently for the children to say the special words.

Today, they were going to learn all about the sea turtles near the Atlantic Ocean off the coast of Florida. Rudi couldn't wait to get there!

The three children closed their eyes tight and happily shouted the words, "GO, RUDI… GO, RUDI… GO, RUDI…"

When they opened their eyes, they saw bright sunshine, a sandy beach, and a beautiful view of the sparkling Atlantic Ocean. They could smell the tang of salt in the air and hear the noise of the rushing waves. Rudi was *so* excited that she ran straight towards the ocean. She was ready to jump in and swim for miles! But she knew that she had to wait for everyone else to join her. Alain, Jazzy, and Krik wanted to make sure that the water was safe for swimming. They were all very good swimmers, but they needed to make sure it was safe. They soon spotted a green flag right next to the lifeguard's lookout. This meant that it was safe for them to swim in the ocean. And it was the perfect day for a swim!

They also saw that there were two lifeguards on duty, keeping the swimmers safe. Before their swim, Jazzy, Krik, Alain, and Rudi decided to investigate the beach to see what they would find. As they began to explore, they suddenly saw some posts that were wrapped in orange tape. On the tape were the words "Do Not Enter!" How curious, they thought. Why were they forbidden to enter *that* part of the beach? They went closer and noticed a sign that read, in big bold letters, **"The Sea Turtles Will Be Hatching Soon. Do NOT Disturb!"**

Wow! They had *never* seen sea turtles before, although Jazzy had read about them in school. It would be so wonderful if the four of them could see some baby sea turtles, known as "hatchlings," hatch and make their way into the ocean. But would they be allowed to?

One of the lifeguards made her way over to the group. She greeted them with a friendly smile and said, "Hi, kids, my name is Lara, and I'm one of the lifeguards here. My friend Carina is the other lifeguard. Welcome to our beautiful beach!"

Jazzy introduced everyone to Lara, and they all quickly became friends. Lara asked the children if they wanted to learn about the flags by the lifeguard post and the ones next to the sea turtles' nest. The three children nodded eagerly. They wanted to know *all* about the beach and, of course, the sea turtles.

Lara began by explaining to them about the different coloured flags that were raised every morning by the lifeguard post. Jazzy, Krik, and Alain had already noticed that the day's flag was green. Lara said that the green flag meant that it was safe to swim in the ocean.

"But even when the flag is green, swimmers must always obey the lifeguard's warnings," she said. "The yellow flag usually goes up when there is a high surf and some dangerous currents. Swimmers need to be very careful then." Lara explained that the red flag was a very serious warning and that no one should swim because it was far too dangerous. The black flag meant **NO SWIMMING AT ALL!**

Rudi was listening to Lara carefully. She understood that everyone always had to be extra careful in the ocean.

"You all picked the best day for the beach," exclaimed Lara. "It's warm and sunny, and perfectly safe for swimming. Go and enjoy, everyone! I'll tell you more beach stories later."

Rudi was impatient. She couldn't wait to jump into the water. The three children—and Rudi—ran down to the ocean's edge, and within a few minutes, everyone was splashing around and having fun. But after everything that Lara had told them, they were all extra careful in the water.

Lara joined them again after they finished their swim. It was time for lunch, and everyone was so hungry! While they ate, Lara said that she was going to teach them all about sea turtles. She knew a lot about them because she had lived near the ocean her whole life and was studying to become a marine biologist. Krik, Jazzy, Alain, and Rudi listened closely as Lara began her story.

"Sea turtles are sometimes called 'marine turtles,' and there are seven species of sea turtles found in many parts of the world, except for the Arctic Ocean and the Antarctic Ocean. There is one species known as the 'flatback turtle,' which lives only in the waters of Australia.

"Sea turtle shells are made of thick plates called 'scutes.' The turtle cannot live without these scutes because they provide protection for the turtle's body. Adult sea turtles travel thousands of miles in the water until they reach their nesting spot. The sea turtles then go ashore to lay their eggs.

"The female turtle digs a hole in the sand and deposits around one hundred eggs. She then covers them up with sand and returns to the ocean. After about two months, the eggs hatch, and at night, the tiny hatchlings make their way from the sandy beach into the ocean. The natural light of the horizon guides the baby turtles towards the water. The hatchlings travel at night because it is safer for them. Larger animals cannot see them or hunt them for food."

Rudi and the children loved Lara's story. They hoped that she would continue to teach them all about the sea turtles. Suddenly, Lara turned to them and whispered, "Guess what? I'm pretty sure that the baby turtles are about to hatch. It's going to be pretty dark soon. If you all promise to be very quiet, we can go and watch them."

The three children nodded excitedly. They were going to see the sea turtles after all! Lara and the other lifeguard, Carina, led the small group as close to the enclosed spot as possible. They all sat patiently and quietly as they waited for the hatchlings to emerge from the sand. Suddenly, the baby turtles began to break free from their shells and carefully make their way out of the sand. One by one, the little hatchlings began to waddle towards the ocean.

Jazzy was thrilled! She whispered to the others, "They're so tiny. Just look at them."

"They can fit in the palm of your hand now," Lara said. "But they will grow to be over four feet long and will weigh over five hundred pounds!"

Everyone watched as the baby hatchlings made their way carefully into the ocean to begin their new marine life. The tiny turtles looked very happy to be out of their shells and very eager to start their new ocean adventure.

The day at the beach had been so much fun, but it was time to go home. The children whispered their goodbyes to Lara and Carina and thanked them for their amazing beach adventure. They had all learned so much about the beach, the safety rules for swimming in the ocean, and, of course, the awesome sea turtles.

Jazzy, Krik, and Alain closed their eyes tight and repeated the special words, "GO, RUDI... GO, RUDI... GO, RUDI..."

When they opened their eyes again, they were all back in the treehouse. It was time for supper. Alain said goodbye after supper and thanked Krik, Jazzy, and Rudi for including him on their beach adventure. He told them that it had been the best day he had *ever* had!

CHAPTER 5

Argentina and the Penguins

The summer was going by quickly. Jazzy, Krik, and Rudi still had many places to visit and explore. They were enjoying their imaginary adventures so much, and they loved learning about new animals, people, and places.

Ever since they were little, Jazzy and Krik had loved learning about penguins. They even had a few penguin posters taped to their bedroom walls. Jazzy especially loved the stuffed penguin toy that she had received as a birthday gift when she turned three. Krik did not have any penguin toys, but he did have many books about penguins that he read over and over again.

Everyone was very excited about that day's trip. Their imagination was going to take them all the way to South America, to a country called Argentina. There they would learn all about penguins and their natural habitat.

After breakfast, Jazzy, Krik, and Rudi went outside and climbed into the treehouse. They settled themselves comfortably on the soft cushions. It was going to be a long trip! They closed their eyes tight and happily shouted,

"GO, RUDI... GO, RUDI... GO, RUDI..."

Jazzy was the first to open her eyes. She excitedly told Krik and Rudi to open their eyes too. What a view! It was unbelievable! They had *never* seen so many penguins before! The children and Rudi had travelled to the very southernmost point of Argentina, which faced the South Atlantic Ocean where it was wintertime and *very* cold.

After getting their bearings, the three travellers decided to take a walk and explore their beautiful new surroundings. They simply could not believe how many penguins they were seeing! After a few minutes, they saw a sign off in the distance, which said, "Welcome to Punta Tombo—Home of Argentina's Friendly Penguins." Jazzy and Krik knew that everyone in Argentina spoke Spanish. They did not know how to speak Spanish, but they were hoping that they would find one of Mommy's friends. Her name was Graciela. She was from Buenos Aires, the capital of Argentina, and she worked in Punta Tombo as an environmental scientist. Mommy had told Jazzy and Krik all about Graciela. She explained that Graciela had lived in Argentina her whole life and had met Jazzy and Krik once when they were very young. What a nice surprise it would be to meet again in Punta Tombo! Mommy had told them that Graciela was studying many features of the environment and was researching different kinds of penguins. Her research was all about how penguins breed and adapt to their natural habitat.

"Graciela wanted to make sure that the penguins of South America were protected and safe and would continue to live healthy lives," Mommy had also said. Jazzy, Krik, and Rudi were very excited to meet her! She would be able to teach them *all* about penguins.

As they continued to walk, Krik noticed a young girl standing next to a woman who was talking to her about penguins. Both were wearing bright red jackets, sunglasses, woolen hats, and warm boots. They were standing on a bridge overlooking Punta Tombo and were pointing excitedly at the penguins.

"Maybe that woman is Graciela," said Krik.

At that exact moment, from the corner of her eye, Graciela spotted a friendly dog happily running in circles around two children. She immediately recognized Jazzy and Krik from the many photos that their mommy had sent her over the years. Graciela began waving excitedly and calling their names. She and the young girl started to head in their direction, both smiling from ear to ear.

"What a wonderful surprise," said Graciela.

Jazzy, Krik, and Rudi were smiling too. They were so happy to have found her! Graciela quickly introduced them to her niece, Karnie, who was learning all about penguins for a school science project. They hugged each other and then decided to get some hot cocoa. It was really cold! Graciela went to find some warm jackets for Jazzy and Krik to wear.

After they warmed up a bit, Graciela said that she would teach them all about Argentina and its amazing penguins. She was very happy that Karnie would be joining Jazzy, Krik, and Rudi on their excursion to visit the penguins.

Karnie is such a friendly girl. I'm sure they will all become friends very quickly, thought Graciela.

After they finished their hot cocoa, they walked over to the Punta Tombo Reserve where there were many penguins. It was an amazing place. Built on the shoreline, the reserve was a sanctuary for penguins.

"Punta Tombo is a long and narrow peninsula," Graciela explained. "It's known for its massive colony of Magellanic penguins. Alongside the penguins, there are other wildlife here, including Patagonian hares, foxes, gulls, dolphins, and whales."

Welcome To Panta Tombo!

Krik wanted to know more about Argentina, its animals, and its people. Graciela loved teaching youngsters about her homeland, as well as its penguins. She happily began to tell the children and Rudi all about life in South America.

"Brazil is the largest country in South America, and Argentina is the second largest. Argentina covers most of the southern peninsula. There are two countries to the north—Bolivia and Paraguay. Brazil, Uruguay, and the South Atlantic Ocean are to the east, and Chile is to the west. Since Argentina is in the southern hemisphere, its seasons are the exact opposite of Canada's, which is in the northern hemisphere."

Graciela went on to explain that the winter months in South America were June, July, and August. "That is why you are seeing so many penguins now," she said.

Everyone became very excited when Graciela mentioned the penguins. She began to teach them many interesting facts about penguin life.

"Did you know that there are seventeen different species of penguins, each one slightly different? All of the penguin species live in the southern hemisphere. Most penguins live on islands, which have very few land predators. That is important for their safety. Penguins cannot fly, so it is very hard for them to escape from danger.

"Although they cannot fly, they *do* have very powerful flippers, making them excellent swimmers. Penguins are known to be the fastest swimming and deepest diving species of bird. They can stay underwater for up to twenty minutes at a time, catching and eating different kinds of fish and other sea life."

While Graciela was talking, Rudi became very impatient. She so wanted to go and play with the penguins! Krik asked Graciela if penguins were afraid of people. Graciela told him that penguins had no fear of humans and often approached groups of people. Even so, Graciela warned them all not to get too close. She wanted the penguins to feel safe.

Rudi listened carefully and obediently stayed with the group. After a few minutes, she noticed a family of penguins starting to make their way over to where she was standing. They seemed interested in the four-legged, furry creature they had never seen before. Rudi decided to be on her best and friendliest behaviour for her new penguin friends. She certainly did not want to frighten them! Jazzy and Krik were proud of Rudi and her excellent behaviour. The penguin family came closer and almost instantly became part of the group. Graciela had never seen anything like it before.

Karnie, Jazzy, and Krik got as close to the penguins as they could. They looked at their interesting markings, their powerful flippers, and their very sharp beaks. Jazzy and Karnie wanted to know more about the baby penguins. They were adorable, and all they wanted to do was play!

Graciela explained, "Newborn penguins are called 'chicks' or 'nestlings.' The female penguin will lay either a single egg or two eggs. Both parents will then take turns holding the eggs between their legs to keep them warm.

"It takes about three and half months for the eggs to hatch," she continued. "Penguins nest in the winter. The females go to the ocean to feed while the male penguins keep the eggs warm."

Graciela, the three children, and Rudi stood for a while longer, watching the many penguin families swimming happily in the frigid waters of the South Atlantic Ocean. Soon enough, it was time for Jazzy, Krik, and Rudi to say goodbye to their new friends and return home.

Jazzy and Krik hugged Graciela and Karnie and invited them to come and visit them in Canada during *their* summer holidays. They thanked Graciela for their amazing day and waved goodbye. Jazzy and Krik took one last look at the penguins, closed their eyes tight, and repeated the words,

"GO, RUDI... GO, RUDI... GO, RUDI..."

When they opened their eyes, they were back in their treehouse. They were filled with wonder at everything they had seen and learned in Argentina with Graciela, Karnie, and of course, the penguins. They could not wait to tell Mommy and Daddy all about their new penguin friends!

CHAPTER 6

Australia, Kangaroos, and koala bears

Jazzy and Krik were always looking for ways to spend time with their cousins during the summer holidays. The next morning, they asked Mommy and Daddy if their cousins could come over for a sleepover. They were planning to pitch a big tent in the backyard and enjoy a fun night of games, storytelling, and lots of popcorn! Of course, they were *also* going to be taking their next imaginary journey from their treehouse. But this time, their cousins would be joining them! On their next trip, they were going to visit kangaroos and koala bears in Australia.

Jazzy and Krik decided to invite Sipana and Sevana, two adventurous sisters who often went camping with their parents, Alexander and Isabella, who always loved to come over for a visit, and Natalie and Alex, who really loved Rudi and now had a puppy of their own named Cosmo. Cosmo was almost one year old and had *a lot* of energy. He was always running around and playing.

"What about Rosie and Oscar?" asked Jazzy. "They are a little bit young for these kinds of adventures, but they could still have lots of fun with all of us, right?"

Krik readily agreed that their cousins Rosie and Oscar should be invited too. Everything was set!

✳ ✳ ✳

Around dinnertime, the cousins began to arrive. Everyone was excited about the backyard sleepover. Rudi was especially excited because she loved having the cousins over. She was also very happy that Cosmo would be joining them too. They would soon be taking a wonderful trip to Australia! Rudi couldn't wait to see the kangaroos and koala bears, but she worried that little Cosmo might not behave himself on the trip. *He's going to get so excited when he sees the animals,* Rudi thought. She decided to keep a close eye on him throughout the trip to make sure that he behaved himself.

The cousins arrived for the sleepover with their overnight bags and lots of snacks and goodies for everybody to share. After supper was over, they all gathered in the backyard. As the sun set, they told stories, ate popcorn, and played games. Everyone was so excited about their Australian adventure the next morning that they could hardly sleep!

Jazzy, Krik, Rudi, Cosmo, and the cousins woke up very early the next morning. After breakfast, they all climbed eagerly into the treehouse. Jazzy and Krik made sure that everyone was comfortable. They packed the treehouse with lots of soft pillows, tasty snacks, and plenty of books about kangaroos, koala bears, and Australia. They were ready to go!

Soon, Jazzy, Krik, and the cousins closed their eyes tight and said the special words,

"GO, RUDI... GO, RUDI... GO, RUDI..."

They opened their eyes and looked around. What a wonderful sight! They were on a ferry boat heading for Kangaroo Island, an Australian wildlife paradise. Kangaroo Island has many beautiful beaches, mountains, deserts, and bushlands. It even has some amazing rock formations that they could see providing they had enough time after visiting the kangaroos and koala bears.

Jazzy, Krik, and the cousins could hardly wait to get to Kangaroo Island! The ferry boat they were on was full of excited tourists eager to see the

kangaroos and koalas. Rudi and Cosmo were also very excited. They hoped that the kangaroos and koalas were friendly, and that they would be able to get close enough to play with them. What fun it would be to make friends with kangaroos and koala bears, they thought.

After a short ride, the ferry boat docked at Kangaroo Island. Everyone left the boat and got into small groups. Jazzy, Krik, and the cousins were in a small tour group called the "Jumping Joeys." Their tour guide was a lovely Australian lady named Nora. Nora was very happy to meet her group and was excited to have Rudi and Cosmo join them. Nora knew instantly that both Rudi and Cosmo were smart and obedient dogs.

The group then boarded a small blue and white tour bus. The words "Welcome to Kangaroo Island" were written on the back of the bus with a picture of "mommy and baby" kangaroos. The bus was the perfect size for the group. It even had enough seats for Rudi and Cosmo!

After everyone was comfortably settled in their seats, Nora passed around some sandwiches and drinks. She also made sure that Rudi and Cosmo's bowls were filled with cold and delicious water. As they ate, Nora began to speak.

"Hello, everyone," Nora said with a warm smile. "Welcome to Kangaroo Island. I know that you are all going to have a wonderful time learning about our beloved kangaroos and koala bears."

Nora then began to tell them more about Kangaroo Island. "It is off the mainland of southern Australia, and it is the third largest island. It has a beautiful coastline, mountains, bushlands, and deserts."

The scenery was beautiful, with the sparkling blue ocean and the mountains off in the distance. Nora told them that their excursion would take place mostly in the bushlands where they would see many kangaroos and koalas in their natural habitat.

The tour bus soon arrived at the wildlife park. There were over one hundred and fifty species of Australian wildlife there, Nora explained. From their seats, everyone caught an amazing glimpse of some kangaroos hopping around. It was incredible!

"Kangaroos and koala bears are marsupials," Nora said. "That means that they are the type of mammal whose babies are born *before* they are fully developed. They then continue to grow in the pouches on their mothers' bellies. Female koala bears keep their babies in their pouches until they are fully developed.

"The baby koala is known as a 'joey,'" Nora continued. "Joeys will not fall out of their pouches because the mother koalas use their strong muscles to keep their pouches closed tight.

"Koalas are easily recognized by their stout, tailless bodies and large heads with round, fluffy ears and large, spoon-shaped noses. Their colours range from silver-grey to chocolate brown, and they love to eat eucalyptus leaves, even though these leaves do not have much nutrition. Koalas also don't move around a lot and sleep up to twenty hours a day."

"That's amazing!" exclaimed Sevana. "But what about the kangaroos?"

Nora smiled and began to tell them all about the kangaroos of Kangaroo Island. "The female kangaroo has a pouch on her belly, just like the koala

bear. This pouch is used to cradle the baby kangaroos, which are also called joeys. When they are born, joeys are only the size of a grape," she said.

"Wow!" exclaimed Alex. "That's *really* tiny!"

Nora continued with her story. "After they are born, joeys travel with their mothers in the safety of their pouches. Kangaroos live in small groups known as 'troops' or 'herds,'" she explained.

Soon after, the bus stopped. It was time to leave the tour bus and go exploring! They were going to see some kangaroos and koala bears up close near some eucalyptus trees. But they had to be very careful, Nora warned.

"Although kangaroos and koalas are friendly animals, humans must always be respectful of them and their natural habitat, especially when they are protecting their young," she said.

Nora then guided her group, with Rudi and Cosmo in the lead, towards the small grove. The children were each carrying some eucalyptus leaves to feed to the koalas, who were all happily basking in the warm afternoon sunshine. The children also held some flowers, ferns, and leaves for the kangaroos.

Jazzy, Krik, and the cousins could not believe that they were so close to actual kangaroos and koala bears! They got as near as they safely could while Nora explained that kangaroos have powerful hind legs and large feet. They also have muscular tails used for balance. The children, Rudi, and Cosmo definitely wanted to stay as *far* away from those powerful legs and tails as possible!

Then, the most amazing thing happened. Nora and the children could not believe their eyes when a mommy kangaroo hopped right up to where they were standing. She was carrying a tiny baby in her pouch! The wee joey peeked her head out and stared in wonder at Rudi and Cosmo with big, golden-brown eyes. She was so excited to have found some new playmates! All she wanted to do was play with everyone. What an incredible moment it was for them all.

It soon became time for them to get back on the tour bus and return to the ferry dock. What an adventure it had been! On the way, they drove

past the huge rock formations. They saw the gigantic boulders perched high above the sea. They had a bright, orange colouring.

"These rocks were formed centuries ago and are famous for their unusual shapes and sizes," Nora explained. "These formations are a collection of granite rocks that have been around for over five hundred *million* years."

"What an incredible thing to see," Jazzy said. The other children definitely agreed with her.

They arrived back at the ferry dock just in time to head back to the mainland on the last ferry boat. The children hugged and thanked Nora for their wonderful tour of Kangaroo Island. They promised her that they would be back again soon.

Once they were safely settled on the boat, Jazzy and Krik told their cousins that it was time for them all to return home. They closed their eyes tight and repeated the words,

"GO, RUDI... GO, RUDI... GO, RUDI..."

When they opened their eyes, they were once again back in Jazzy and Krik's treehouse. Sipana, Sevana, Alexander, Isabella, Natalie, Alex, Rosie, and Oscar agreed that the sleepover and the exciting adventure in Australia had been the best time they had ever had! Rudi agreed. She could not *wait* for the next journey. She hoped that the cousins, and Cosmo, would be able to join them again too!

CHAPTER 7

Egypt and the Camels

The night before their next adventure, Jazzy asked Krik if he had any books about Egypt and the pyramids. Krik said that he had one book that their grandmother had given to him on his last birthday. It was a beautiful book, large and golden, with a picture of Queen Nefertiti on the cover.

"Nefertiti had been the Queen of Egypt many centuries ago," explained Krik. His book was full of colourful pictures and interesting facts about Egypt's ancient kings and queens. And the pyramids.

"That's definitely the right book to take with us tomorrow morning on our next imaginary trip to Egypt," said Jazzy.

Krik readily agreed. "Let's also bring some maps and information that I will download tonight from the Internet," said Krik. "Then we will have everything we need to learn all about Egypt's pyramids, camels, kings, queens, and the River Nile!"

The next morning, everyone got up early. Jazzy, Krik, and Rudi were so excited for their Egyptian adventure to begin! As always, Rudi made sure that she was well prepared for the trip. After breakfast, the three of them ran outside and climbed into the treehouse. They brought all of the books, maps, information, water, and goodies that they needed for their journey to Egypt. Rudi was especially glad that they had also brought a lot of water. It was going to be a hot day, and the cold water would be so refreshing!

Jazzy and Krik closed their eyes tight and said the special words,

"GO, RUDI... GO, RUDI... GO, RUDI..."

When they opened their eyes, Krik yelled, "Jazzy, look! We are so close to the pyramids!"

Jazzy looked over to where Krik was excitedly pointing. Sure enough, there stood the grand pyramids. The children and Rudi had arrived in Egypt! They immediately saw that they were surrounded by desert sand, huge monuments, happy tourists, and many camels. Some of the tourists were even *riding* on the camels! There was much to see and do.

From their books, maps, and Internet research, Jazzy and Krik knew that Egypt was situated close to the equator and that countries that were located just above or below the equator had a very *hot* climate all year round. Jazzy and Krik had also learned that the equator was actually an imaginary line that went around the middle of the earth and was halfway between the North Pole and the South Pole.

"The equator divides the earth into its northern and southern hemispheres," Jazzy explained. "Egypt is located in the northern hemisphere." Jazzy had learned all about it in her geography class at school. She was very proud to share her knowledge with Krik and Rudi.

"Boy, is it ever hot," Krik exclaimed. "Good thing we're wearing our sunhats and brought lots of water!"

In the distance, the children spotted a group of students, who were busily clearing a small area. They were all carrying small brushes, maps, and digging tools.

"Do you think they are looking for buried treasure?" Krik laughed.

"They are digging for ancient artifacts and bones," replied Jazzy excitedly. "That is sort of a buried treasure, Krik!" The children were thrilled that they

were going to see an actual archaeological excavation. They had only ever seen those in the movies.

Jazzy, Krik, and Rudi approached the small group of student diggers. With the group were two teachers, who were busily answering questions and giving out instructions. Jazzy and Krik had many questions too. They wanted to know what the students were looking for and what was buried underneath the hot sand.

As they came nearer, one of the students approached and introduced herself. "Hi, my name is Nafisa. Would you like to help us with our excavation?"

Jazzy and Krik eagerly accepted her offer. What a learning experience it would be! Imagine what they could find!

Nafisa told them that she and her friends were archaeology students from a nearby university. She then described to them a bit about her work. "Archaeologists study human history by digging up artifacts, such as prehistoric tools, animal bones, and different kinds of relics from centuries ago. The sites we work on are called 'digs.'"

Jazzy and Krik had so many questions for Nafisa. She knew that she had done the right thing by inviting them to help out on the dig.

"Once we are done digging and had our lunch, how would you like it if I gave you all a tour of the pyramids? You may even get the chance to ride on a camel before you leave Egypt," Nafisa said.

The children could not believe their luck! They happily accepted Nafisa's kind offer. Rudi was even more excited than Jazzy and Krik. She had never even seen a camel before. Now she was going to be *riding* on one!

Jazzy and Krik joined Nafisa and the other archaeology students on their dig. It was very hot, and soon, everyone was sweating and thirsty. *This is really hard work,* thought Krik.

All of a sudden, Rudi stuck her nose into the ground and began to dig frantically with her two front paws. To their amazement, she suddenly uncovered a huge bone! The others began to dig even deeper around Rudi's find, and soon enough, they discovered even *more* bones.

"What kind of bones are they?" asked Jazzy.

One of the teachers explained that the bones probably belonged to an animal that had lived in Egypt centuries ago. "We are going to take these bones and examine them very carefully back at the university. Then we will know what kind of animal this is and how old it is," said the teacher. Everyone was absolutely thrilled with the discovery of the bones.

"We couldn't have done it without you, Rudi!" Nafisa said happily.

Jazzy and Krik were proud of Rudi. Rudi was proud that what she had done had made everyone *so* happy.

After lunch, the archaeology students and their teachers said goodbye to Jazzy, Krik, and Rudi. They thanked them again for all of their help on the dig. Then Nafisa, Rudi, and the two children left to explore the great pyramids.

"Did you know that the pyramids of Egypt are considered one of the Seven Wonders of the World?" Nafisa asked. "The three great pyramids were built four thousand five hundred years ago in the city of Giza, and each pyramid has its own name. The Pyramid of Khufu is the oldest and largest, followed by the Pyramid of Khafre, and the Pyramid of Menkaure.

"The pyramids were built by the ancient Egyptians, and it took them over twenty years to build each pyramid. Their bases are squares and their sides are triangles."

"What were the pyramids used for?" asked Krik. Nafisa smiled at his clever question.

"The Egyptians built the pyramids as tombs for their pharaohs and queens. The most famous pyramid was built for Pharaoh Khufu. It stands almost four hundred and sixty feet high. The pyramids also symbolized power and strong religious beliefs. Inside the pyramids, there are lots of pictures on the walls, which are called 'hieroglyphs.' This ancient Egyptian language describes the daily lives of the kings and queens of Egypt," Nafisa explained.

The children and Rudi looked admiringly at the pyramids while Nafisa continued her story.

"The Egyptians knew that it was wise to build the pyramids close to the River Nile because it was easier for the builders to transport the massive stones to the building site by boat. The River Nile is also the longest river in the world. It runs throughout Egypt and creates a fertile valley for the growing of crops along the desert."

"But what about the Sphinx? What does it mean?" asked Jazzy.

Nafisa replied, "The majestic pyramids are guarded by the Great Sphinx of Giza, which stands in front of them. The Sphinx is a statue of a mythical creature with the body of a lion and the head of a human. It is one of the oldest, largest, and most famous statues in the world."

After their tour of the pyramids, Nafisa guided them over to the camels. They were going to ride the camels after all! As Jazzy, Krik, and Rudi excitedly prepared for the ride, Nafisa explained that camels were comfortable in the hot, dry weather of Egypt.

"Their thick coats are made of a type of hair that protects them from the sun, and they have wide, soft feet that help them to walk for long distances on the desert sand. Camels also have three eyelids and two rows of eyelashes, which prevents the sand from entering their eyes. The camels' humps are not used to store water but fat, which is used by the camels for energy. They can survive for a long time without water, and very thirsty camels can drink up to one hundred litres of water *at one time.*"

Finally, it was time for them to ride the camels. *Boy, are they ever tall,* thought Krik. Nafisa had already explained to them that camels were almost seven feet tall! Jazzy and Krik climbed up on their camels' backs while Nafisa helped Rudi up on the camel that they would be sharing. They rode their camels slowly by the ancient and majestic pyramids. It was the most incredible experience!

As the sun began to set over the desert, their ride was over. It was time for Jazzy, Krik, and Rudi to return home. They hugged Nafisa and thanked her for all that she had taught them about archaeology, the pyramids, the geography of Egypt, and the camels. What an extraordinary learning experience it had been for them all.

Jazzy and Krik waved a final goodbye to Nafisa. They were ready to go home. They closed their eyes tight and repeated the special words,

"GO, RUDI... GO, RUDI... GO, RUDI..."

When they opened their eyes, they saw that they were once again back in their treehouse. What an amazing day it had been! Jazzy and Krik yawned tiredly as they entered the house, but Rudi was wide awake. She could not stop thinking about her camel ride with Nafisa!

CHAPTER 8

Armenia and the Storks

The summer holidays were almost over, but Jazzy and Krik still had *one* more place to visit before heading back to school. They both agreed that it was important for them to learn more about the country where their great-grandparents were born. They would be visiting the beautiful country of Armenia. Jazzy and Krik were going to learn about many historical sites, travel to Lake Sevan and Mount Ararat, and get to know more about the country's famous storks.

"I read somewhere that the stork is a well-known bird in Armenia," said Krik.

"Well, there should be plenty of them there!" answered Jazzy excitedly. They both knew that Rudi was going to love learning about the storks too.

The night before their last imaginary journey of the summer, Jazzy and Krik carefully prepared their maps and books. They made sure that everything was packed and ready for their Armenian adventure. Growing up, they had heard a lot about Armenia from their parents and grandparents.

They also spoke Armenian fluently. They were so excited for their trip that neither of them could sleep.

Early the next morning, Jazzy, Krik, and Rudi quickly finished their breakfasts and ran outside to the backyard. They climbed into the treehouse, carrying their books, maps, and some snacks for the trip. They looked at each other excitedly. They were ready to go!

The children closed their eyes tight and happily yelled out the words, "GO, RUDI... GO, RUDI... GO, RUDI..."

When they opened their eyes, they saw that they were in Yerevan, the capital of Armenia and one of the world's oldest cities. Jazzy, Krik, and Rudi were standing right in the middle of the main city area known as "Republic Square." They were surrounded on all sides by beautiful historic buildings. There was so much hustle and bustle going on around them that they could not believe their eyes!"It's so busy!" exclaimed Jazzy.

Everywhere they looked they saw cars and buses, happy children on their way to school, noisy street vendors selling fresh fruits and vegetables, and street artists painting beautiful floral scenes. The sidewalk cafés were full of people, and the delicious aroma of freshly brewed coffee filled the air. Jazzy and Krik had never seen such a vibrant and exciting place!

The children then began to look for a young woman named Lenya. Her parents and Jazzy and Krik's parents were great friends. Lenya was going to be their tour guide for the day and would be taking them to many different places. She would also be teaching them all about the country of Armenia.

"Is that her, Jazzy?" asked Krik.

"I think it is."

The two children had spotted a pretty, young woman standing alone in the middle of the noisy square. They began to wave at her to get her attention. Lenya saw them and immediately recognized them. She had seen many family pictures of Jazzy, Krik, and especially Rudi. The three hugged each other and laughed. It was as though they had known each other all their lives! Rudi was happy to have found a new friend.

"The four of us are going to have the most amazing day," said Lenya. "I'm going to teach you many wonderful and exciting things about Armenia."

Jazzy and Krik looked at each other happily. They knew that Lenya had been born in Yerevan and understood the language, culture, and history of Armenia really well. She was also very organized and had their entire day all planned out. They couldn't wait to get started!

Soon after, Lenya, the two children, and Rudi boarded a minivan. The driver of the minivan announced that they were heading to Lake Sevan. During the ride, Lenya pointed out to Krik and Jazzy many famous historical sites. She also began to teach them about Armenia and the Armenian people.

"Armenia is proud to be the first nation to adopt Christianity as a religion. That is why the country has so many old monasteries and churches. It's amazing to think that many of these churches were built centuries ago and high up on mountaintops," Lenya explained. "One of the most beautiful of these monasteries is the Tatev Monastery, which was built on the top of a mountain!"

"That's really amazing," said Jazzy.

"If we visit the monastery, we can ride the cable car down to the village of Halidzor," said Lenya. "It is called the 'Tatev Aerial Tramway' and it's in *The Guinness Book of World Records* as the world's longest, non-stop, double-track cable car."

"Wow!" Krik exclaimed. "That is so cool!"

Lenya asked Krik and Jazzy if they knew how to play chess. They both answered that their father had been teaching them the game.

"Did you know that chess is taught in all Armenian schools starting from a very young age?" asked Lenya.

"I guess that explains why Armenia always wins chess championships," said Krik. "The best chess player in the world is from Armenia!" Jazzy and Krik decided then and there to start playing chess with their classmates when they returned to school.

The minivan was almost at Lake Sevan. The drive had been very scenic and pleasant along several winding roads.

"After lunch, we will all be going on a boat ride. I'll also tell you lots more about Armenia," Lenya promised with a big smile. She had a huge surprise planned for Jazzy and Krik.

They soon arrived at the lake. The minivan stopped and everyone got out. The sight that met their eyes was incredible.

"Lake Sevan is so beautiful!" Jazzy exclaimed. She had seen many pictures of it in her grandparents' photo albums, but this was truly amazing. There were many people in the lake swimming, windsurfing, or jet skiing.

Lenya, the children, and Rudi found a quiet spot under a shady tree and started to have their lunch. Suddenly, Jazzy and Krik heard their grandparents calling to them from a distance. They could not believe their ears! Jazzy, Krik, and Rudi excitedly ran over to where their grandparents were standing.

"Grandma! Grandpa!" the children shouted joyfully. "What an incredible surprise!"

Grandma and Grandpa hugged their grandchildren tightly. They had not seen them for a very long time.

"Come and join us for lunch," said Krik. They happily agreed, and soon, everyone was comfortably settled underneath the shady tree. As they ate their lunch, Jazzy and Krik told their grandparents all about the sights they had seen in Armenia so far. Lenya watched the happy group and smiled. She was pleased that her surprise had turned out well. Rudi sat extra close to Grandma and Grandpa. She was so happy to see them too!

All of a sudden, Jazzy heard another familiar voice approaching them. She turned to see who it was and saw *another surprise!* There stood Karnie, the young student they had met in Argentina! Karnie was in Armenia visiting family, she told them. Jazzy and Krik quickly introduced her to Lenya and their grandparents and invited her to join them on their boat ride. Rudi was so happy that Karnie was going to be joining them. She remembered how nice Karnie and her auntie Graciela had been to her in Argentina.

It was time for the boat to depart. They climbed aboard and set sail on beautiful Lake Sevan. Lenya told them that there would be one more surprise on their trip back to the city. *What could it be?* they wondered. The children could hardly wait to find out.

After a lovely and scenic boat ride with the grandparents and Karnie, it was time for them to head back to the city. On the minivan, Lenya told them all her wonderful surprise.

"We are going to stop at Mount Ararat and take a tour of the base of the mountain!" she said. "Mount Ararat is known as the 'resting place' of Noah's Ark. It is also a very important national symbol for Armenians."

Krik wanted to know more about the mountain. Grandpa explained that Mount Ararat consisted of two peaks—Greater Ararat and Little Ararat, or Masis.

"Many mountain climbers have reached the peak of Greater Ararat, which is almost seventeen thousand feet high," Grandma explained.

The children were so excited! Stopping at the base of Mount Ararat would be another highlight of their trip. They could hardly wait to get there!

Jazzy then asked Lenya if she would tell them about the stork, Armenia's favourite bird.

"White storks often nest close to people, including on rooftops and on telephone poles," said Lenya. "Many Armenians believe that a stork's nest on their house is a sign of good luck! Even though Armenia is a small country, more than three hundred and fifty bird species live here. It's very important to keep all of these birds safe from extinction."

Lenya continued with her story, "Every year, from March to August, hundreds of storks settle into their nests. There they hatch nestlings and teach their babies to feed. Armenia has the perfect climate and environment for storks. It is their 'stop over' country on their long journey south to Africa.

"The reason storks are so loved by everyone is because there have been many stories, passed down from one generation to the next, about storks bringing newborn babies to families."

Jazzy, Krik, and Karnie smiled knowingly. They had heard those stories too.

Slowly, the minivan approached Mount Ararat. Karnie exclaimed that she could see the peak of the beautiful mountain! Jazzy and Krik looked excitedly out of the van's windows. They too spotted the majestic mountain. It was just as glorious as they had imagined it to be.

The minivan stopped at the base of the mountain. Lenya began to sing Armenian songs, and Karnie started to dance. Naturally, Jazzy, Krik, and their grandparents joined in the fun as Rudi jumped and skipped around them. It was just like a party! And Rudi so loved parties!

It had been the most incredible day. The children had seen and learned a lot about Armenia, Lake Sevan, Mount Ararat, and the storks. But it was time for Jazzy, Krik, and Rudi to return home. After they all hugged each other tightly, they promised that they would all meet up again in Armenia soon and climb Mount Ararat all the way to the top!

Jazzy and Krik wished that they could stay in Armenia with their grandparents and friends a bit longer. But they knew it was time to go home.

The two children, with Rudi by their side, closed their eyes tight and repeated their happy words for the very last time that summer,

"GO, RUDI... GO, RUDI... GO, RUDI..."

When they opened their eyes, they were once again back in their tree-house. Jazzy and Krik looked at each other and smiled. What an amazing and unforgettable summer it had been with all of their imaginary trips and adventures. They had learned so much about so many wonderful places, animals, and people. The summer holidays were over, and it was almost time to return to school.

Rudi looked lovingly at Krik and Jazzy. She would never forget the best summer she had *ever* had.

The End

Lightning Source UK Ltd.
Milton Keynes UK
UKHW050208250521
384260UK00011B/37